Mumble Bear

by GINA RUCK-PAUQUÈT

illustrated by ERIKA DIETZSCH-CAPELLE

translated by Anthea Bell

G. P. Putnam's Sons · New York

"Mumble Bear is a dear bear," said the animals.
"Mumble Bear is a kind bear."
"Mumble Bear will do anything you ask him to do."
Mumble Bear is a quiet bear. He only mumbles.

Mumble Bear would have liked to spend his time playing the violin and dreaming, but the other animals would not leave him alone. They always wanted him to do things for them.

"Brush my fur, Mumble Bear," said Francis Leo Pard. Francis Leo Pard was very proud because he had two first names. All the rest of his family were only called Leo.

Mumble Bear brushed Francis Leo Pard's fur.

"Look after my babies, Mumble Bear," said Moony Owl.

Moony Owl woke up only when the moon was full. The rest of the time she slept.

Mumble Bear looked after the baby owls.

"Run, Mumble Bear!" said the Pincher Monkeys. "We want to ride on your back."

And they pinched and nipped Mumble Bear. Mumble Bear ran.

"Make me a nest, Mumble Bear," said the Tree Rhinoceros.

The Tree Rhinoceros was a special Rhino who liked to sleep in the treetops.

Mumble Bear made him a nest and tucked him in.

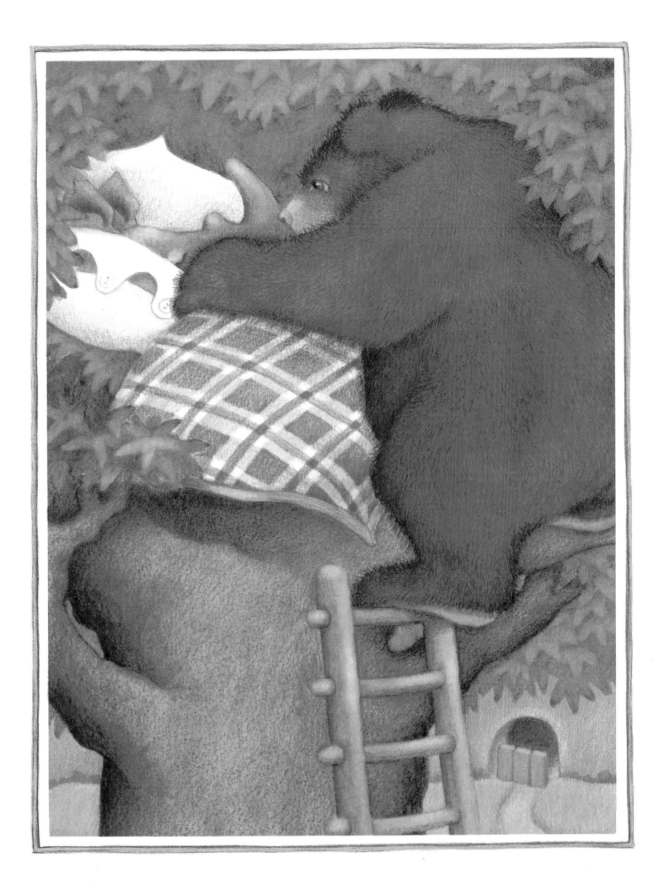

"Sing me a lullaby, Mumble Bear," said Fizzymouse. "I want to go to sleep in your pocket."

Fizzymouse was called Fizzymouse because she loved fizzy drinks.

Mumble Bear sang her a lullaby.

"Come and dance with me, Mumble Bear," said the Prancing Dancing Camel.

And he swept Mumble Bear into his prancing dance, and stepped on Mumble Bear's toes.

Mumble Bear was a kind bear. He did whatever the other animals wanted, all day and every day.

He did what Francis Leo Pard wanted.

He did what Moony Owl wanted.

He did what the Pincher Monkeys wanted.

He did what the Tree Rhinoceros wanted.

He did what Fizzymouse wanted.

He did what the Prancing Dancing Camel wanted.

But Mumble Bear never did any of the things *he* wanted to do.

Mumble Bear was an unhappy bear.

He began to feel smaller and smaller. Even smaller than Fizzymouse. So Mumble Bear took his violin and went off to hide in his cave.

But he couldn't play and he couldn't dream.

"Come out, come out!" cried the animals.

"Who's going to brush my fur?" asked Francis Leo Pard.

"Who's going to look after my babies?" asked Moony Owl.

"Who's going to give us rides?" asked the Pincher Monkeys.

"Who's going to sing me a lullaby?" asked Fizzymouse.

"Who's going to let me step on his toes?" asked the Prancing Dancing Camel.

"I will," mumbled Mumble Bear.
Because Mumble Bear was such a dear bear.

But, at night, in his dreams, Mumble Bear was a mean bear. He was big and bad and fierce with cruel sharp teeth. He even dreamed he ate up Moony Owl.

But luckily that was only a dream.
So Mumble Bear kept doing whatever the other animals wanted him to do.

Until one day, Mumble Bear had had enough.
He wouldn't do what Francis Leo Pard wanted,
or Moony Owl, or the Pincher Monkeys, or the
Tree Rhinoceros, or Fizzymouse.

Now Mumble Bear was not a dear bear.
And he was not a mean bear.
Mumble Bear was just Mumble Bear.

Mumble Bear went off to his cave.
He played his violin.
And he dreamed his dreams.

"What lovely music he plays," whispered the other animals. "Mumble Bear is a wonderful bear!"

From then on,
    they brushed their fur,
        watched their babies,
            built their nests,
                sang their lullabies,
                    danced their dances,
                        by themselves.

And Mumble Bear was their friend.